...e pictures and often tells stories, all of it magic and all of it true.

...tures and all of the stories, and all of the magic, the music is you.

— John Denver —

GUEST DEDICATION

To children the world o'er who have to lie on a hard floor or scramble to be fed—some day
may you all sleep on a Feather Bed. — Jim Connor, songwriter of "Grandma's Feather Bed,"
band member and long-time friend of John Denver

ILLUSTRATOR DEDICATION

For Navona — Christopher Canyon

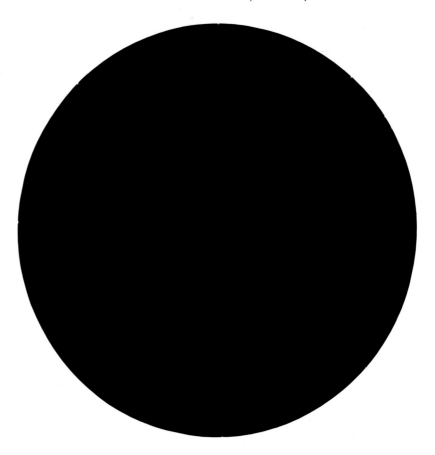

ACKNOWLEDGEMENTS BY THE PUBLISHER

Many thanks to children's literary agent Sandy Ferguson Fuller of Alp Arts Company, who, while John Denver was alive, conceived the i[...]
spirit to children through picture books, and after his passing pursued it to fruition; also to Hal Thau, John's long-time friend an[...]
Jim Bell of Bell Licensing; and Michael Connelly and Keith Hauprich of Cherry Lane Music Publishing Company.

Dawn Publications
12402 Bitney Springs Road
Nevada City, CA 95959
www.dawnpub.com

Book Design by Christopher Canyon.
Production and prepress by Christopher Canyon and Patty
Arnold.
First Edition
10 9 8 7 6 5 4
Manufactured by Regent Publishing Services, Hong Kong,
Printed May, 2016, in Guangdong, China

Library of Congress Cataloging-in-Publication Data

Canyon, Christopher.
 John Denver's Grandma's feather bed / adapted and illustrated by Christopher[...]
   p. cm.
 Summary: A picture book adaptation of the song written by Jim Connor, and m[...]
which celebrates the fun of visiting grandmother's house. Includes facts about G[...]
grandparents, and their music.
 ISBN 978-1-58469-095-5 (hardcover) -- ISBN 978-1-58469-096-2 (pbk.)
 1. Children's songs--United States--Texts. [1. Beds--Songs and music. 2.
Family life--Songs and music. 3. Grandmothers--Songs and music. 4. Songs.]
I. Denver, John. II. Connor, Jim, 1938- Grandma's feather bed. III. Title.
IV. Title: Grandma's feather bed.
 PZ8.3.C1925Jmg 2007
 782.42--dc22
 [E]
                                         2007015120

pictures and often tells stories, all of it magic and all of it true. tures and all of the stories, and all of the magic, the music is you.

— John Denver —

GUEST DEDICATION

To children the world o'er who have to lie on a hard floor or scramble to be fed—some day
may you all sleep on a Feather Bed. — Jim Connor, songwriter of "Grandma's Feather Bed"
band member and long-time friend of John Denver

ILLUSTRATOR DEDICATION

For Navona — Christopher Canyon

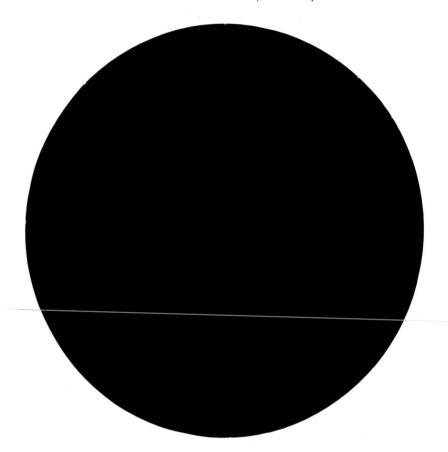

ACKNOWLEDGEMENTS BY THE PUBLISHER

Many thanks to children's literary agent Sandy Ferguson Fuller of Alp Arts Company, who, while John Denver was alive, conceived the ide
spirit to children through picture books, and after his passing pursued it to fruition; also to Hal Thau, John's long-time friend and
Jim Bell of Bell Licensing; and Michael Connelly and Keith Hauprich of Cherry Lane Music Publishing Company.

Dawn Publications
12402 Bitney Springs Road
Nevada City, CA 95959
www.dawnpub.com

Book Design by Christopher Canyon.
Production and prepress by Christopher Canyon and Patty
Arnold.
First Edition
10 9 8 7 6 5 4
Manufactured by Regent Publishing Services, Hong Kong,
Printed May, 2016, in Guangdong, China

Library of Congress Cataloging-in-Publication Data

Canyon, Christopher.
  John Denver's Grandma's feather bed / adapted and illustrated by Christopher C
    p. cm.
  Summary: A picture book adaptation of the song written by Jim Connor, and mad
which celebrates the fun of visiting grandmother's house. Includes facts about Cor
grandparents, and their music.
  ISBN 978-1-58469-095-5 (hardcover) -- ISBN 978-1-58469-096-2 (pbk.)
  1. Children's songs--United States--Texts. [1. Beds--Songs and music. 2.
Family life--Songs and music. 3. Grandmothers--Songs and music. 4. Songs.]
I. Denver, John. II. Connor, Jim, 1938- Grandma's feather bed. III. Title.
IV. Title: Grandma's feather bed.
  PZ8.3.C1925Jmg 2007
  782.42--dc22
  [E]
                                                        2007015120

John Denver's
Grandma's Feather Bed

Adapted & illustrated by Christopher Canyon

Dawn Publications

When I was a little bitty boy

just up off the floor,

we used to go out to Grandma's house
every month-end or so.

We'd have chicken pie and country ham
and homemade butter on the bread,
but the best darn thing about
Grandma's house was her
great big feather bed!

It was nine feet high and six feet wide,
soft as a downy chick.
It was made from the
feathers of forty-'leven geese,
took a whole bolt of
cloth for the tick.

It'd hold eight kids,
four hound dogs,
and the piggy we stole
from the shed.

We didn't get much sleep but we had a lot of fun on Grandma's feather bed!

After supper we'd sit around the fire,
the old folks'd spit and chew.
Pa would talk about the farm
and the war

and my Granny'd sing a ballad or two.
I'd sit and listen and watch the fire,
till the cobwebs filled my head.

Next thing I'd Know
I'd wake up in the morning
in the middle of the
old feather bed.

It was nine feet high and six feet wide,
soft as a downy chick.
It was made from the
feathers of forty-'leven geese,
took a whole bolt of
cloth for the tick.
It'd hold eight kids,
four hound dogs
and the piggy we
stole from the shed.
We didn't get much sleep
but we had a lot of fun on
Grandma's feather bed!

Well I love my pa, I love my ma,

I love Granny and Grandpa too.

I've been fishin' with my uncle,

I wrassled my cousin,

But if I ever had to make a choice,
I guess it ought to be said,
I'd trade 'em all, plus the gal down the road,
for Grandma's feather bed.

It was nine feet high and six feet wide,
soft as a downy chick.
It was made from the
feathers of forty-'leven geese,
took a whole bolt of
cloth for the tick.
It'd hold eight kids
and four hound dogs
and the piggy we
stole from the shed.
We didn't get much sleep
but we had a lot of fun on
Grandma's feather bed!

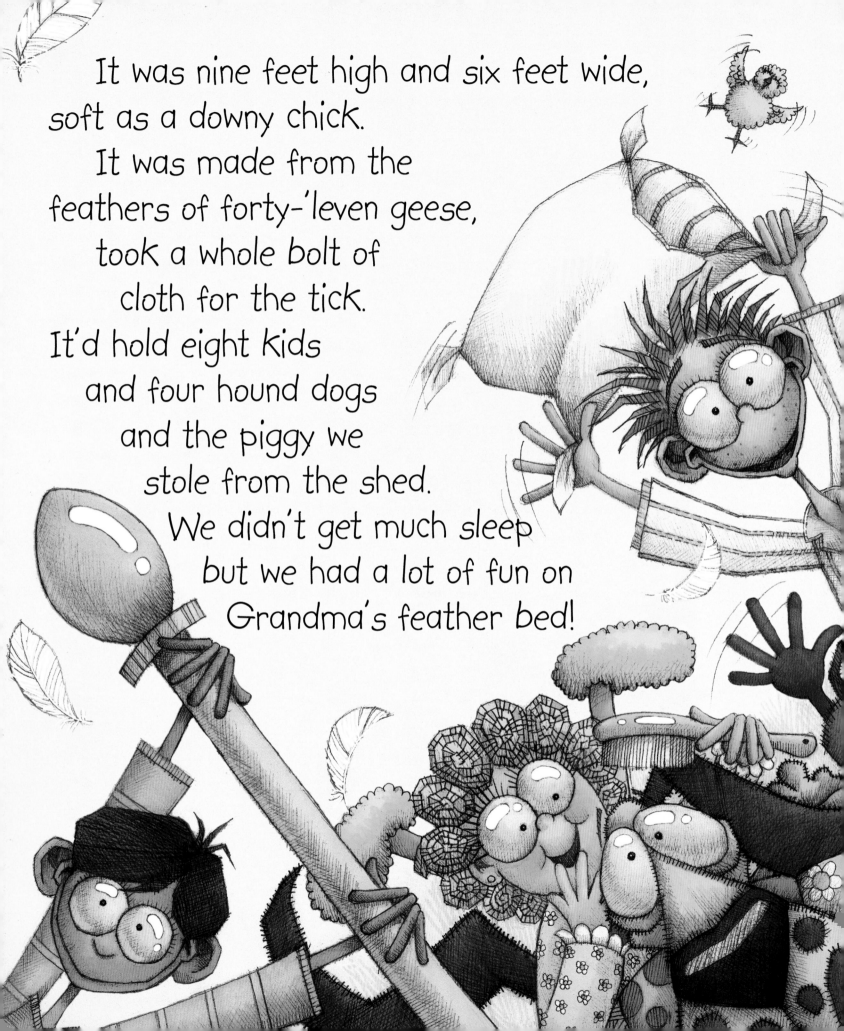

We didn't get much sleep but we

had a lot of fun on Grandma's feather bed!

Jim Connor and John Denver

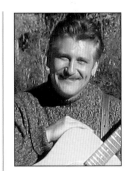

"Grandma's Feather Bed" was written by Jim Connor, a renowned banjo player, and "adopted" by John Denver. John and Jim were friends, and around the holiday time in 1968, before skiing, Jim sang the little ballad. John had a tiny cassette recorder with him, and captured it on tape. "John heard something in my little ballad to my Granny that even I didn't see," Jim says, "and kept it in his heart until he found the opportunity to sing it to the whole world." John said the song reminded him of good times with his paternal Grandma and Grandpa, who had eleven children, ten of them boys! John said:

I remember the old family farm in Oklahoma, a bed full of kids and so many quilts on top of us that we couldn't move. I remember all of the family around the kitchen table and rooms filled with laughter and climbing through the rafters in the attic. I remember how excited I would get the closer [I got] to the farm, and how much I loved being there and how much I hated to leave when we would have to go. All of that and more is captured in this song. I was going to write this song. Jim just beat me to it. Thanks, Jim! I couldn't have written it any better.

The granny that it honors is Jim's Grandma Florence Setzer of Birmingham, Alabama. The photograph on the right was taken in 1964 at the Great Southern Folkmusic Jamboree where Florence, 86 years old, sang ballads of Appalachia, accompanied by her grandson Jim on the banjo. Earl Scruggs once called Jim "the finest living banjo player, and perhaps the best that ever lived."

And who was Aunt Lou? She was Grandma's daughter, Louise. In 1975, Aunt Lou attended a John Denver concert at the huge Coliseum in Birmingham. John invited her to come on stage as he, Jim and the band performed "Grandma's Feather Bed." John and Jim often performed the song together on stage. But Aunt Lou would have none of it. She said, "Why, I ain't going to get up there and embarrass myself in front of 20,000 people!"

John loved to sing about such things as feather beds, sunshine, and country roads—good, life-affirming songs. And he used his celebrity status—over 32 million John Denver albums were sold in the U.S. alone—to campaign vigorously for humanitarian and environmental causes.

Christopher Canyon spent much of his childhood growing up in rural Ohio where he spent most of his time drawing, playing guitar and singing songs with his family. In his youth, Christopher was deeply influenced by the music of John Denver. "John's songs gave me hope, joy, and an unbounded belief in possibilities," he says.

Christopher is an award-winning artist, musician and performer dedicated to sharing the joy and importance of the arts with children, educators and families. He frequently visits schools, providing entertaining and educational programs, and is a popular speaker at conferences throughout the country. "Everyone has what it takes to be artistic, and it's not talent. It is our creativity," he says. "As humans we are all creative beings and our individual creativity is one of our most powerful gifts. If we celebrate and use our creativity in positive ways it is amazing how much we can learn, how much we can discover and how much joy we can share."

This is the tenth book Christopher Canyon has illustrated for Dawn Publications, including the earlier books in the "John Denver & Kids" series. He lives in historic German Village in Columbus, Ohio with his wife Jeanette Canyon, also a well-known children's book illustrator.

ALSO IN THE
JOHN DENVER & KIDS SERIES

Sunshine On My Shoulders

Ancient Rhymes: A Dolphin Lullaby

Take Me Home, Country Roads

Dawn Publications is dedicated to inspiring in children a deeper understanding and appreciation for all life on Earth. To review our titles or to order, please visit us a www.dawnpub.com, or call 800-545-7475

Grandma's Feather Bed

Jim Connor